RACER

M.G. HIGGINS

SADDLEBACK
EDUCATIONAL PUBLISHING

red rhino b**OO**k s™

With more titles on the way …

SADDLEBACK
EDUCATIONAL PUBLISHING
www.sdlback.com

ISBN-13: 978-1-62250-893-8
ISBN-10: 1-62250-893-9
eBook: 978-1-63078-025-8

Printed in Guangzhou, China
NOR/0714/CA21401177

18 17 16 15 14   1 2 3 4 5

Austin Jackson

Age: 11 (getting taller every day)

Best School Subject: science

Favorite Food: pancakes with grape jelly

Most Embarrassing Secret: sleeps with a teddy bear

Best Quality: honesty

Slice

Age: 12 (big for his age)

Favorite Movie: *Big*

Future Plans: create a BMX clothing line

Secret Wish: to have an older brother and a younger sister

Best Quality: endurance

1
NIGHTMARE

I'm going fast. Maybe too fast. I tap the brake. Lean into the corner. My foot scrapes the dirt. Somehow I stay upright. Out of the turn I pump my legs again. Only one rider is ahead of me. It's Slice. I recognize his red mountain bike. The red stripes on his helmet. If I can beat him, I'll win.

I get closer. Rocks fly from his tires. One

last hill and dip. Then the finish line. My legs burn. My lungs ache.

Now I'm even with Slice. I glance over. He looks back at me and scowls. *Yeah, it's me*, I feel like saying. *You're about to lose to little Austin Jackson.*

We're on the last hill. He speeds up. So do I. I reach the top ahead of him. All at once my back tire jumps. The next second, I'm flying off my bike, screaming.

I sit up in my sleeping bag, panting. My pj's are wet with sweat. The tent is quiet. I must not have yelled. Or Mom and Dad would be hovering. Asking if I'm okay. I'm sick of these nightmares. My accident happened over a year ago. But it still feels like yesterday.

I unzip my bag. Throw on my clothes. Open the tent flap. Step outside. The sun is just coming up. It turns the sky orange. Lightens the nearby hills. I rub my arms. Even with my hoodie, I'm freezing. The desert is so cold at night. And then hot during the day. Weird.

From the cooler I grab a juice box. Down it in a few gulps. I scarf a granola bar. My brothers' bikes lean against the van. My chest tightens when I see them. I used to love riding. Loved racing. But after two broken legs. A broken arm. A month in the hospital. I decided I'm never riding again. Ever.

I grab my backpack. Cram a water bottle inside. Head for the trail.

"Austin?"

I turn. Dad's sticking his head out the tent. "You okay?" he asks.

I roll my eyes. "Yes."

"Did you have a bad dream?"

I take a deep breath. I don't answer.

He looks at me. Then he says, "Don't go too far. Stay within shouting distance. And watch for snakes."

"Yeah, Dad. I know."

He frowns. Slips back inside the tent. He's not happy I'm going out on my own. But he knows I need to get away. I hate watching them gear-up to ride. It makes me feel sorry for myself. It also makes me jumpy. Scared.

Before   after

I fling my pack over my shoulder. I don't care about riding anyway. I have a new hobby. Mom and Dad got me a rock tumbler for my birthday. Seeing dull old rocks turn shiny? Awesome. A year ago I was Austin Jackson, mountain-bike racer. Now I'm Austin Jackson, rock collector.

"Awesome," I mutter.

2
OFF LIMITS

I trudge along a hiking trail. Climb a hill. The campground spreads below me. There are loads of campers and trailers. Only a few tents like ours. Dad says he likes using a tent. But he'd buy a camper if we could afford it. I also see tons of bikes. It's Saturday. The first race weekend of the spring. My older brothers, Jeb and Cal, are practicing today. Tomorrow they race.

Something red catches my eye. An RV is just pulling into the campground. It's as big as a bus. I feel my jaw clench. It's Slice. Everything his family owns has that fire-engine red stripe. The RV. The car the RV is towing. Slice's bike and gear.

I grip the strap of my backpack. Quickly climb down the hill.

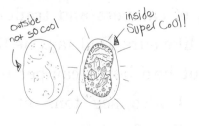

Dad said to stay close. But I'm not. I like it in these hills. I can't see bikes. Or hear bikers. Plus, it's a good place to find rocks. Today I'm hunting for geodes. Geodes are pretty cool. On the outside they're plain balls of brown. But inside? They might be full of crystals. You don't know until you open them. I'm also on the lookout for turquoise. Or maybe I'll get really lucky and find a fossil.

Within a few hours, I've only found two geodes. A few other rocks might polish up nice in the tumbler. But no turquoise. No fossils. That's not a very good haul. I want to hunt some more before I head back for lunch. The trail meets up with an old dirt road. I see a metal sign.

WILDLIFE PRESERVE
PROTECTED AREA

NO BIKES
OR VEHICLES
BEYOND THIS POINT

There are threatened animals around here. Plants too. They explain all that when you sign up to race. You're not supposed to go off the bike trails. But I'm on foot, so I should be okay. I pass the sign. Take a long drink from my water bottle. I see cactus and shrubs. Wildflowers. This area is really beautiful.

It's late morning. Warming up already. I start to pull off my hoodie. Hear something. A sound I know like my own heartbeat. It's a bike. And it's going fast, passing me. I yank off my hoodie. I only have time to see the rear of the bike. A helmet. They swerve around a hill.

There was red on that helmet. Was it Slice? If so, what was he doing here? I start to run. I follow the tire tracks. I get around the hill. The biker is long gone. I stop, out of breath. Slice isn't the only rider who wears red. But the shade I saw was bright. Fire-engine. The more I think about it, the more certain I am. It was Slice.

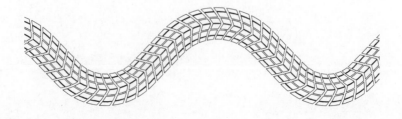

I don't want to tattle. But Slice shouldn't be riding off-trail. It's against the rules. Cheating. I need to tell someone. I start to head back to camp. As I near the sign, I see a brownish-gray lump. I noticed it before, when I chased after the biker. I thought it was just a rock. But this rock is moving.

3
SUSPECT

A tortoise! I've only seen them in photos and on TV. It's about the width of a basketball. Maybe as tall as my ankle. I stand still. I don't want to get too close. I know how it feels to be scared. It rises on its stocky legs. Starts to walk. Then stumbles. It quickly sinks to the ground. I don't know a thing about tortoises. But that does not look right.

same width

"Hey, fella," I say. "You okay?"

I take slow steps toward it. It tucks its head into its shell. Only its beak-like nose sticks out. I think that's how tortoises protect themselves. They can't run. So they pull into their shells. The shell acts like a bike helmet.

I've closed in. I can make out small details in its shell. That's when I see the crack. It's about two inches long. Above the tortoise's front leg. The shell has started to split. That can't be good.

Ouch!

"Hey, little guy." I feel like I need to give it a name. *Geode* pops into my head. "So, Geode. What happened to you?"

He doesn't move.

I look around. About a foot away I see bike tracks. They're fresh. They must have come from Slice's bike. He was really zooming when he passed me. Did he hit Geode? Knock him so hard his shell cracked?

I don't know. I do know the tortoise needs help. He's not walking right. Maybe he has other injuries too. Like when I had my accident. My liver was bruised.

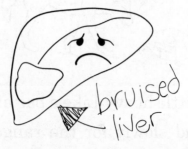

bruised liver

"Darn it, Slice," I say. My anger builds up again. I clench my fists. How could he do this? He should not have been riding out here.

The ranger station isn't far. It's near the park entrance. I saw it when we drove in. I could run there in a few minutes. But I don't want to leave Geode behind. What if Slice comes roaring back? What if a coyote finds him? I gently slide my fingers under Geode's bottom shell. I lift him off the ground.

He's a little heavy. Like a bag of groceries. We head slowly for the ranger station. The whole way I think about Slice. I started racing when I was nine. I was smaller than Slice. I also wasn't as strong. He always beat me. He teased me too. Called me *Little*

Austin. *Wimp*. *Loser*. But after I turned eleven, I had a growth spurt.

I showed up for this race a year ago. Slice saw me and dropped his jaw. I'd grown. He hadn't. Now we were the same height. I would have won that race. But he kicked my bike. He almost killed me. He denied it. I couldn't prove it. But I know. And he knows.

The ranger station comes into view. I look down at Geode. He hasn't moved. I want Slice to pay for this.

4
CRIME

I've walked for thirty minutes. My arms are about to fall off. Geode has gotten heavier with each step. I climb slowly up to the ranger station. The tortoise doesn't look any worse. But he doesn't look any better.

I walk inside. A blast of cold air hits me. Man, I love air-conditioning. There's a woman behind the counter. Otherwise the place is empty. She sees me. Then she sees

Geode. Her eyes narrow. "Young man. What are you doing with that tortoise?"

"He's injured," I say.

Her face softens. "Oh. Bring it here."

I set Geode on the counter. "His shell is cracked." I point.

"I see. Where did you find it?"

"Not far from the campground. In the protected area. I was hunting for rocks."

She squints again. Looks Geode all over. He still hasn't peeked his head out.

"Do you know how it happened?" she asks.

"I think a bike hit him."

"You saw this?"

I shift my feet. "Well. Not exactly."

"What *did* you see?"

I tell her about hunting for rocks. About a biker zooming by. Then finding Geode and the tire tracks.

"You named him Geode?" She smiles.

"Yeah. It didn't seem right calling him an *it*."

"Well, just to let you know. Geode is a *she*." She points at its rear. "I can tell by her tail. And the shape of her lower shell." She looks at me. "What's your name?"

"Austin."

"I'm Joy." Then she says, "So, Austin. You didn't see the tortoise … Geode … get hit. But did you see who rode by?"

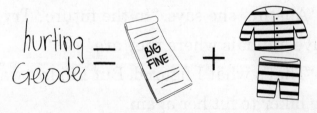

I think it was Slice. I'm almost positive it was him. But I'm not completely sure. And I don't want to lie. Crud. I take a deep breath. Shake my head. "No. Not really." Then I ask,

"Is what happened a crime?"

"Sure is. Desert tortoises are a threatened species. Harming one can result in a very big fine. Even jail time."

"Wow."

"Thank you for helping Geode," Joy says. "We'll have a vet check her out."

"Will she be okay?"

"As long as she's not hurt inside. Cracked shells are not too hard to fix."

"Thanks." I turn to leave.

"Austin," she says. "In the future? Try to leave animals where they are."

"That's what I figured. But I didn't want the biker to hit her again."

"I understand."

I give Geode and Joy a small wave.

I walk toward the campground. I've just noticed how hungry I am. It's way past lunchtime. Mom must be wondering where I am.

Way Past lunchtime

In the distance I hear yelling. Cheering. I see bikes soar over the hills. Clouds of dirt fly into the air. I think I see Jeb and Cal. Then I catch a glimpse of fire-engine red. I grip the straps of my backpack. I lower my eyes. Walk a little faster.

Joy said hurting Geode could result in a big fine. Jail time. I wish I could prove it was Slice.

I take a deep breath. Maybe I can.

5
SNOOP

Mom *was* worried about me. I feel kind of bad. She gives me a hug. Then she grips my shoulders. Looks me in the eyes. "Austin. Do not be gone so long again. I was about to get a ranger."

"I was just at the ranger station."
"You were?"

I tell her all about Geode.

"You could have found me," she says. "I would have driven you."

"Maybe next time."

She shakes her head. "I wish our phones worked out here." She starts making tuna sandwiches. "I'm taking lunch to your dad and brothers. Then I thought I'd watch them ride." She eyes me. "Want to come along?" she asks cheerfully.

Why is she even asking? Of course I don't. I chew the sandwich she puts in front of me.

She pats my shoulder. Then she puts food in a small cooler. "I'll be back in two hours.

I want you to stay in the campground. You can read that book you brought. Okay?"

"Sure. Fine."

It *is* fine. This is just where I want to be. I have some snooping to do.

I head out as soon as Mom leaves. It's not hard to find Slice's campsite. That red RV is hard to miss. I walk by it all casual. Like I'm out for a stroll. I'm not sure what I'm looking for. I figure I'll know it when I see it. Or hear it. Maybe I'll overhear Slice confess to what he did. Now I wish I had a tape recorder.

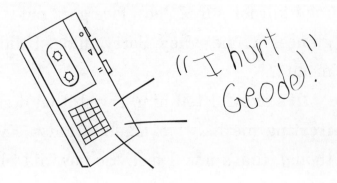

I walk past their campsite. Turn around. Walk back. The place looks deserted. No people. No bikes. Which makes sense. They're at the race. This was a dumb idea. There's no evidence here. I walk back to my campsite.

It's late afternoon. Jeb and Cal have just come back from riding. It kills me to listen to their stories.

"Did you see my final hill?" Cal says to Jeb. "I can't believe I pulled that off."

"I know," Jeb says. "I thought you'd be road kill for sure." Jeb's face goes pale. He glances at me. "Hey. Sorry, dude. I didn't mean ..."

"It's okay," I tell him. I wish they'd stop treating me like I'm made of glass. Even though that's how I feel. "So how did Slice

28

do?" I need to change the subject. And maybe get some useful info.

FRAGILE

PLEASE, HANDLE WITH CARE

Jeb shrugs. "Front of the pack. But I don't know how he did it."

"What do you mean?" I ask.

"He started in the back. Didn't see him for a while. Then he showed up out of nowhere. He was in front."

Huh. I think I know how he did it. A shortcut. Right through the protected area. Seems like someone would have seen him. But it's a long route. And there are so many hills and turns. It's up to riders to be honest.

After dinner I stretch my arms. "I'm bored. I'm going for a walk."

"Want some company?" Dad says.

"Nah. Just going around the campground. I'll be back soon."

I head to Slice's campsite. I'm surer than ever he's to blame. I just need a few more pieces to lock this puzzle into place.

6
CLUES

It's getting dark. I throw on my hoodie. Grab my flashlight.

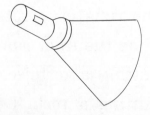

No one is outside Slice's campsite. You'd think with this big RV he had a big family. But it's just him and his parents. A silver light flickers through a window. Must be a TV.

Slice's bike leans against the RV. It's near the front door. I creep closer. Nice bike. Expensive. I may not ride anymore. But I still feel a pang of envy. On a hunch, I crouch. Look at the tires. I've seen lots of crime shows. Stuff gets stuck in treads. Like plants. A flower from the protected area.

I shine my flashlight on the front tire. Only dirt. Small rocks. I check the back tire. No luck there either.

I study the rims for scratches. There's a big scratch on the front rim. Could have been from hitting a tortoise. Could have been from hitting a rock. I take a deep breath. I'm getting nowhere.

Suddenly I hear voices. I can't make out words. But they're loud. Angry. There's a noise near my head. Someone's opening the door. Crud. I get on all fours. Crawl under the RV.

"Where are you going?" The voice is deep.

Gruff. Must be Slice's dad.

"Nowhere!" It's Slice. He jumps down the steps.

"Do you want to win?" his dad yells. "Then sometimes you have to bend the rules. You do what you have to do!"

"Yeah. Whatever," Slice says.

The door slams. Slice marches off into the darkness. He switches on a flashlight.

I get out of there. Fast.

I wake up with a start. Another nightmare.

I don't go back to sleep.

SUNDAY
√ Bad mood
√ Rock hunting
~~Be a good bro~~

The rest of the morning is a repeat of Saturday. Me in a bad mood. Out rock hunting at first light. I should watch Jeb and Cal race. Be a good brother. But I can't. I just can't.

I go straight to the protected area. It's where I left off yesterday. I still want some good rocks to take home. I try to focus. But I think about Geode. I wonder if she's okay. Then last night's dream plays through my head. So does what I overheard at Slice's RV. His dad told Slice to "bend the rules." A shortcut sure bends the rules. But is that enough evidence to convict Slice? I doubt it.

I shake my head. Try to clear it. To my left is a rocky mound. There could be some interesting rocks in there. Maybe even fossils. I crouch. Brush sand off with my hand. Lean in for a better look.

I hear that sound again. The sound of a bike going fast.

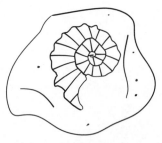

7
SWERVE

I forget about rocks. I jump up. See fire-engine red. Red stripes slashing across the rider's helmet. It's Slice. I have no doubt.

He's coming toward me. What will he hurt this time?

"Hey!" I jump into the middle of the trail. Wave my arms. "Stop!"

He doesn't slow. "Out of my way!" he yells.

I jump off the road at the last second. "Slice! Slow down!" I chase after him.

He nears a hill. It's the place I last saw him yesterday. He goes wide to make the turn. But he's going too fast. His bike goes into a slide. He tries to pull up. But the front tire hits a rock. The bike flips end over end.

So does Slice.

He lands on his head. Then onto his side. He stops in a crumpled heap. He's not moving.

I've seen bad crashes. This is bad.

I run up to him. His arm bends at a weird angle. It must be broken. But I'm mostly worried about his head and neck. He landed so hard. Helmets only do so much.

I crouch next to him. "Slice?"

He doesn't answer. The fall must have knocked him out.

Crud. Now what?

I have to get help. I could run to the campground. But everyone is at the race finish line. The race! There's always an EMT truck standing by. That's where I need to go. But it's too far on foot.

I stand. Search for Slice's bike. It's lodged upside down in a bush. I pull it out. It's banged up. The handlebars are bent. But the rims are good. The tires have air.

I glance around. Look for someone else to get on this bike. To do what I'm too scared to do. But I'm alone. It's up to me.

Every nightmare flashes through my mind. Racing, flying, falling. The terror. The anger. This is *Slice*. The guy who sent me to the hospital. The reason I'm hunting rocks instead of riding. Do I really want to help him?

I glance at his crumpled form. Maybe I don't want to. But I have to. I'd expect him to do the same for me.

I take a deep breath. Swing my leg over the bike. Lightly sit down. Wipe my sweaty palms on my pants. Grip the handlebars.

"Okay. Let's do this."

I slowly push off.

8
RACE

I'm all jitters. The bike shakes. It's like I'm five years old again. Like it's my first time on a bike. I force myself to breathe. To focus. I'm not wearing a helmet. No padding. What if I fall? I need to get to the race site quick. But I need to stay upright.

I pump my legs harder. I watch the

ground. Then I look ahead of me. Nothing fancy. No tricks. I just need to ride.

I build up speed. The jitters start to fade. I'd forgotten how good this feels. The wind against my face. Like I'm free. Like I'm flying.

In a few minutes, I see racers. Now I know why Slice took this shortcut. The trail meets the race route from behind a hill. He timed it right yesterday. No one saw him.

I join the race. Bikers swerve around me. I'm going too slow.

"Hey, watch it!" a racer yells.

I tense up. I fight the urge to stop. To pull

to the side. Instead, I force myself to go faster. Up ahead is the finish line. I see a crowd of people. Dad's baseball cap. Mom's straw hat. And the EMT van.

I cross the finish line. Keep going. "Excuse me," I say, panting. I pedal through the crowd.

"Austin?" Dad says as I ride by. Mom's mouth hangs open.

"Sorry! Can't talk now." I keep moving.

I get to the EMT van. Two techs are leaning against it. They're watching the race.

"Emergency!" I sputter. "In the protected area. Kid fell off his bike. Broken arm.

He's unconscious."

"Where again?" one of them asks.

I point. Tell them how to get there. Then I say, "I'll ride back to him. I'll wave when I see you."

"Good. Thanks." They jump into the van. Start it up. The lights flash.

By now Mom and Dad are next to me. So is Cal. Jeb must still be racing.

"What's going on?" Mom asks.

"Isn't that Slice's bike?" Cal asks.

"Yeah. He took a shortcut. He's injured. I need to get back to him. Can I borrow your helmet and pads?"

Cal shrugs. "Sure." He takes them off. I quickly put them on. He's only a little bigger than me.

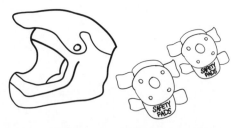

"We'll go with you," Mom says.

"No time," I tell her. "I'll be okay. Will you tell Slice's parents? Maybe they can follow the EMTs."

"We will," Dad says. He gives me a worried smile. "I'm glad to see you riding again. But I'm sorry about what happened. Be careful."

I smile. "Always."

I take off. This time my fear is gone. I ride like the wind. I ride like someone's life depends on it.

9
TRUTH

I get to Slice before the EMTs. It doesn't look like he's moved. I lean over him.

"Slice?" I say.

He moans. Turns his head. I let out my breath. That's a good sign. I kneel next to him.

"My arm hurts," he says.

"I think it's broken. Don't move too much. I rode your bike. I got help. The EMTs are on their way."

Slice's arm

"Thanks." Then he says, "I think I hit a turtle yesterday. Came out here last night with a flashlight. Couldn't find it. Would you look?"

"Already did. And she's a tortoise. She should be okay."

"Good. I'm sorry. Didn't mean to hurt her."

He feels sorry about hitting Geode? He actually looked for her? I think about what I overheard at his RV last night. His argument with his dad. Maybe that's what it was about. Maybe Slice didn't want to take this shortcut. "Sometimes you have to bend the rules," his dad had said. "You do what you have to do."

Slice's dad

"Does your dad pressure you to win?" I ask.

"Sometimes." He winces in pain. "I want to win too. But I want to deserve it. I don't want it from cheating."

I feel the old anger inside. It simmers. Bubbles. Boils to the surface. "What about a year ago? I was about to win this race. You kicked my bike. You almost killed me!"

"No. I didn't." He winces again. "I was mad you were winning. But I didn't touch your bike. Think about it. I was too far away."

I hear an engine. I get up. It's the EMTs. A car with a red stripe follows close behind.

I wave my arms. "Over here!"

In seconds, the techs rush to Slice's side. So does his dad. His face is pale. He looks like he's going to be sick.

I lean Slice's bike against his dad's car. Find my backpack where I left it. Hike toward the campground.

I have a lot to think about. Slice can be a real jerk. But he feels bad about hurting a tortoise. He cheats. But he says he doesn't like to. And what about my accident? I want to blame him. But my gut tells me otherwise. I think he's telling the truth. Maybe he *was* too far away to kick my bike. Maybe my back tire hit a rock. Maybe I was going too fast. Maybe it really was just an accident.

I get to the campsite. The tent is down. Dad and Jeb are folding it. Mom and Cal are packing the van. She looks up and sees me. "Austin." She drops what she's doing. Gives me a big hug. "How's Slice? Will he be okay?"

"Yeah. I think so."

"And how are you?"

"I'm fine, Mom." For once, I think I really mean it.

Dad comes over. "So. Ready to get your bike out of storage?"

"Um. Maybe. I'll think about it."

"Awesome!" Jeb punches my arm.

"Great to have you out there again, bro." Cal rubs my head with his knuckles.

"Hey." I laugh and push his hand away. "But I'm not going to give up rock hunting. I kind of like it."

"Good. You can do both." Mom winks. "I want a necklace from that tumbler."

We drive out of the campground. I see the ranger station. I have some unfinished business. "Dad," I say. "Do you mind stopping? I'll just be a sec."

He pulls the van over. I run inside.

Joy smiles when she sees me. "Hey. It's the tortoise rescuer."

"How's Geode?" I ask.

"The vet just checked her this morning. No internal injuries. He clamped her shell. She should be fine."

"Great." I take a deep breath. I came in to tell her about Slice. That he confessed to hitting Geode. But now I'm not so sure. It won't help Geode any. And I'm pretty sure Slice will stay on the trails from now on. Plus, he has a lot on his plate right now. I know. I've been there.

"Was there something else?" she asks.

"No. Just … tell Geode 'hi' for me."

"I'll do that."

I get back in the van. I can't wait to get home. I've got a bike to clean. And geodes to open.

10
RACE

I see the curve up ahead. Every instinct tells me to slow down. Trees border both sides of the trail. If I hit one, I'll break into a million pieces. But there's only one rider ahead of me. And I really want to win.

I tap the brake. Just a little. My bike starts to slide. My breath catches. I lean away and come out of the curve.

I did it!

I pedal up the next hill. The kid with the blue helmet is a few yards away. I push myself harder. I get closer. But now I hear a biker behind me. Where did he come from? I pump harder. I'm just behind the leader. He crosses the finish line. The kid behind me scoots by at the last second. I come in a close third. Rats!

My family rushes up. Dad pats my back. He's beaming. "Great race, Austin!"

Mom gives me a hug. "That was terrific."

"Not bad." Cal socks my arm.

"I guess I owe you that pizza," Jeb says. He bet me I wouldn't finish better than tenth.

I'm breathing too hard to say anything. I feel bad I didn't win. But this was my first race in over a year. I guess third is okay.

My brothers head to the start line. Their age group is up next.

I search the crowd as I catch my breath. I see them. "I'll be back in a sec." I walk my bike to an RV. A red stripe swooshes across the side.

Slice and his dad lean against the RV.

Slice's arm is in a cast.

"How's the bike?" his dad asks.

"Great. It's a sweet ride. I wanted to thank you again."

It feels strange. I'm riding a bike with a red stripe. But Slice's dad was super happy I helped his son. He gave me one of his pricey bikes. I guess as payment. I miss my old bike a little. But this one really is awesome.

"Good," his dad grumbles. "Um … nice race." He disappears inside the RV. Slice's accident shook him up. But I can tell he hasn't totally changed. He still wants his son racing again. I wonder at what cost.

"I wish I was out there," Slice says. "I would have won."

"I don't know," I say. "That was a tough group."

He gives me a crooked smile. "I would

have beaten you. Like always."

I smile back. "See you at the next race, Slice."

"Yeah. See you … Austin."

I head back to the tent for my rock-hunting gear. I hear there are fossils in these hills. I'm going to find them.